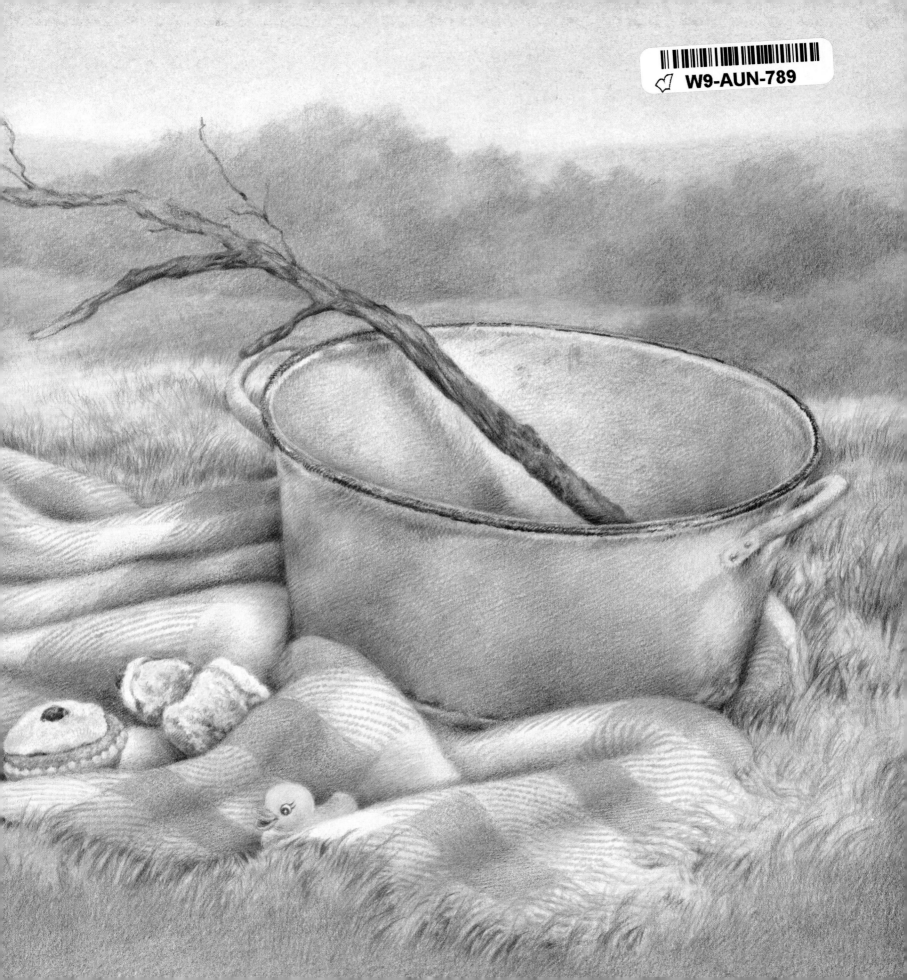

For remembering the best . . .

First U.S. edition 2006

Library of Congress Cataloging-in-Publication Data is available.

Library of Congress Catalog Card Number 2005046924

ISBN 0-7636-2962-6

2 4 6 8 10 9 7 5 3 1

Printed in China

This book was typeset in Berling.
The illustrations were done in colored pencil and pastel.

Candlewick Press
2067 Massachusetts Avenue
Cambridge, Massachusetts 02140

visit us at www.candlewick.com

Hooray for Harry

Kim Lewis

CANDLEWICK PRESS
CAMBRIDGE, MASSACHUSETTS

Harry the elephant wanted a nap.

When he went to lie down, his bed was bare.

His fluffy old blanket just wasn't there.

"Oh!" said Harry. "My blanket is gone!"

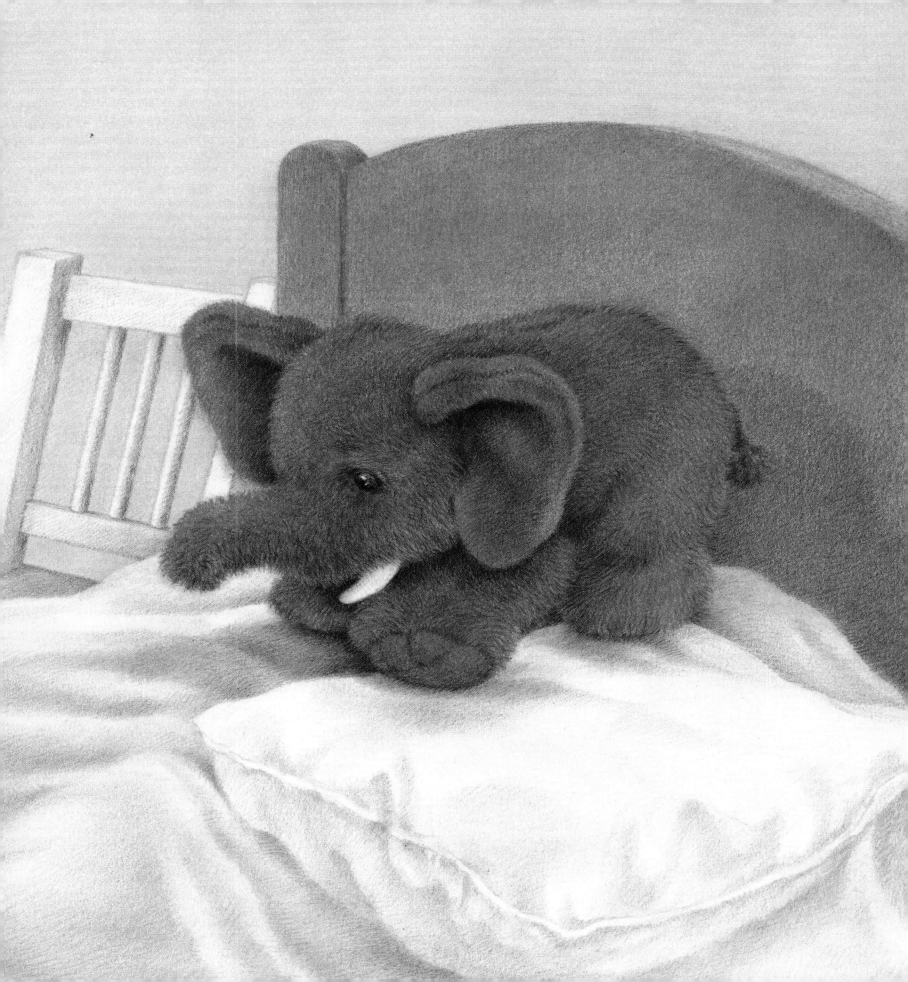

Harry and his friends, Ted and Lulu, started
looking for Harry's blanket.

Harry searched
the cupboard.

Ted emptied
the toy box.

Lulu looked
under the bed.

But the three little friends
couldn't find Harry's blanket.
"Where, oh where,
did I put it?" said Harry.

"Did you leave your blanket outside?" asked Lulu.

Harry thought about it. "Oh!" he cried. "I remember! We made a tent in the long, tall grass. We all crawled in."

"We did!" said Ted.

But when Harry, Ted, and Lulu ran outside,
the blanket tent in the grass had gone.

"What did we do next?"
wondered Lulu.

Harry thought some more.
"We made a sail for my boat!"
he said. "I was the captain
and you were the crew. My
blanket blew in the wind."
"I looked for pirates!" said Ted.

But when the three little friends ran to Harry's boat, there wasn't a blanket sail on the mast.

"Hmmm," said Lulu. "What happened then?"

"We made a swing in the trees!" said Harry.

"We all went *swoop*!" said Ted.

Harry, Ted, and Lulu ran to the trees.

But the trees didn't have a blanket swing.

"We must have done something else. . . ." said Lulu.

Harry tried thinking a little bit more.

"Oh!" he cried. "Now I remember!

We had a picnic in the meadow.

We all sat on my blanket."

"I ate up all my picnic," said Ted.

"My blanket got very sticky. . . ." said Harry.

"I know!" said Lulu. "We washed it!"

The three little friends
ran to the bucket.

"But your blanket's not in here," said Ted.

"My dear blanket," said Harry. "I thought
it would be here. I really did."

"Never mind, Harry," said Lulu. "You'll
remember where it is in a minute."

"Don't worry, Harry," said Ted. "We'll find your blanket. I know we will."

So Harry tried thinking, just one more time.

Harry thought of his blanket, so fluffy and soft.
He thought very hard. He thought and thought.

My blanket was a tent,
then a swing and a sail.
Our picnic made it all
sticky. We washed it
and washed it
and then . . .

What did we do with my drippy wet blanket?

"Oh!" cried Harry. "NOW I REMEMBER!
We hung my blanket up to dry!"

Harry ran as fast as he could to the clothesline.
Lulu and Ted ran after Harry.

And there was the blanket, dancing in the wind,
fresh and clean and waiting for Harry.

"My blanket," cried Harry. "I found you!"

"Hooray for Harry!" cried Lulu and Ted.

"You remembered where it was after all," said Lulu.

"I knew you would," said Ted.

"I'd NEVER forget my blanket," said Harry.

The three little friends cuddled up for a nap.

"I love my blanket," sighed Harry.